We Are in a Book!

To Cher and Trixie,
who are first in my book

ISBN 978-1-338-71459-3

Text and illustrations copyright © 2010 by Mo Willems. All rights reserved. Published by Scholastic Inc., 557 Broadway, New York, NY 10012, by arrangement with Hyperion Books for Children, an imprint of Disney Book Group. ELEPHANT & PIGGIE is a trademark of The Mo Willems Studio, Inc. SCHOLASTIC and associated logos are trademarks and/or registered trademarks of Scholastic Inc.

12 11 10 9 8 7 6 5 4 3 2   20 21 22 23 24 25

Printed in the U.S.A.   40

First Scholastic printing, September 2020

This book is set in Century 725/Monotype; Grilled Cheese BTN/Fontbros; Billy/Fontspring

An ELEPHANT & PIGGIE Book

SCHOLASTIC INC.

4

7

9

13

The reader is reading these word bubbles!

SO COOL!

22

23

If the reader
reads out loud.

Ahem.

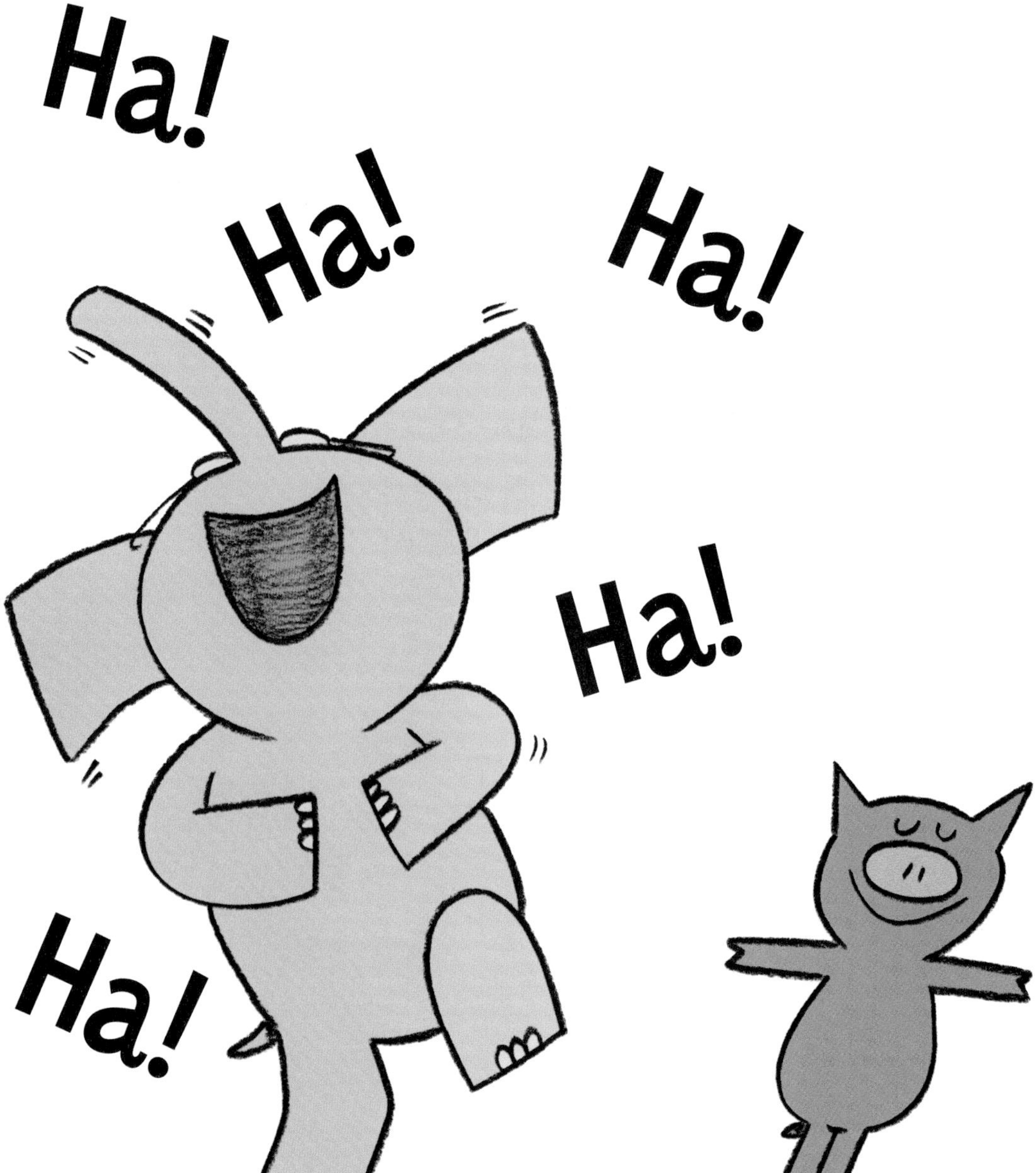
Ha!
Ha!
Ha!
Ha!
Ha!

Hee!
Ha!
Hee!
Ha!
Ha!
Ha!
Hee!
Ha!
Ha!
Ha!
Hee!
Hee!
Ha!
Ha!
Hee!
Hee!
Ha!
Hee!
Hee!
Ha!
Ha!
Hee!
Hee!
Hee!
Ha!
Hee!

Hee!
Ha!
Ha!
Hee!
Hee!
Ha!
Hee!
Ha!
Hee!
Hee!
Ha!
Ha!
Hee!
Hee!
Ha!
Hee!
Ha!
Ha!
Hee!
Ha!

49

57

Have you read all of Elephant and Piggie's funny adventures?